NORMAN

The Demon

Doorman

For Penny
J. W.

For the Wright Family, Klub Barbounia members
K. P.

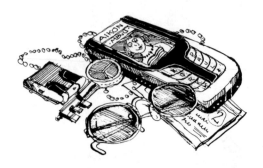

ORCHARD BOOKS
338 Euston Road, London NW1 3BH
Orchard Books Australia
Level 17/207 Kent Street, Sydney, NSW 2000
ISBN 1 84362 159 2 (paperback)
First published in Great Britain in 2004
First paperback publication in 2005
Text © Jeanne Willis 2004
Illustrations © Korky Paul 2004

A CIP catalogue record for this book is available
from the British Library.
1 3 5 7 9 10 8 6 4 2 (paperback)
Printed and bound in China
Orchard Books is a division of Hachette Children's Books

NORMAN
The Demon
Doorman

Jeanne Willis * Korky Paul

ORCHARD BOOKS

NORMAN
The Demon Doorman

Watch it, pal, you can't come in!
I'll have to land one on your chin
If you attempt to jump the queue.
That's why I'm here - that's what I do.

There's a party here tonight,
(Get back! You're asking for a fight!)
Unless your name is on the list
You're not invited - see this fist?

I'm hard as nails. I have to be.
I'm what they call a bouncer, see?
And if my clients hold a bash
I'm paid to keep out any trash.

I work for all the story folk.
You think it's fun? It's not a joke –
That woman who lives in a shoe?
She's one bad mother! Man, it's true!

She held a party for her brats.
Tommy Thin came – watch out, cats!
He had an egg fight, I recall,
And drove poor Humpty up the wall.

The Shoe Kids? They were running riot.
I just couldn't keep them quiet.
They made the mice play Blind Man's Buff
And pinned the tail to a Billy Goat Gruff.

Last Saturday? Well, what a mess!
The guests all came in fancy dress
And folk from forests near and far
All came to visit Grandmama.

Red Riding Hood had baked a cake
With candles on, for Granny's sake.
And Gran was just about to bite...
When somebody snapped on the light.

"That's not Gran!" the Axe Man said.
"Granny's still at home in bed.
It's the wolf! He's in disguise!"
(What big teeth and what big eyes!)

It's not the first time he's been bad.
He claimed he was the Piglets' dad
And blew their bouncy castle down.
I chased him halfway round the town.

I collared him behind a tree
And said, "You're coming back with me.
The bouncy castle needs inflating -
Huff and puff! Come on, I'm waiting!"

The catering can be quite nice
At functions - but I won't eat rice.
A big fat weasel made me stop -
He ate too much and went off pop!

There was treacle everywhere
And little clumps of weasel hair.
I like a sausage-on-a-stick
But rice and treacle make me sick.

I don't like party games. Bo-Peep
Is always up for "Hunt the Sheep".
I've had it up to here with lambs
And bleating ewes and missing rams.

Boy Blue's a one for hide and seek.
I lost the little beast last week.
I found him underneath a stack
Of hay, with Jill - no sign of Jack!

Oh yeah, there was another time
A guest was party to a crime.
I'd say it almost was the worst –
The Miller's daughter's twenty-first.

The DJ had his decks in place.

The Prince was there – Prince What's-His-Face?

Out looking for a Bride-To-Be,

(The Miller's daughter, hopefully).

I thought that it was rather queer
When she arrived with spinning gear.
Apparently, she had been told
To turn the party string to gold.

I said that this was cruel and mean,
But she insisted she'd be Queen
If, while they played "The Birdie Song"
She spun and strung her dad along.

The string turned into golden thread!
"Please dance with me!" Prince Thingy said.
"OK," she smiled. The prince was sweet
But boy, did he have two left feet!

Now everything was going fine
Until some dwarf stepped out of line.
He told me that he was a chum
Of Her Indoors and knew her mum.

I didn't like the look of him -
I knew his brothers. They were grim.
"I don't know who you are," I said.
"So tell me, is it Frank or Fred?"

He said I'd have to guess his name.
I bellowed at him, "What's your game?
I haven't time for stupid riddles -
Is it Tom, or Tim, or Tiddles?"

"Is it Bill, or Bob, or Bert?
Answer me, you little squirt!
Does it start with A or B?"
The midget bit me on the knee!

He pushed right past me in a flash.
The spinning wheel fell over...smash!
He kicked it with his little welly.
Whooops! He skidded on a jelly.

He crashed into the disco lights.
The prince tripped up and tore his tights.
The King choked on his pipe and he
Was leapt on by the fiddlers, three.

Just then, over the Karaoke
I heard a voice – it sounded croaky.
It was the Frog Prince doing Rap –
"I know the name of the little chap!"

"Yo! He's wicked! Yo, he's thin!
He's all rumpled! He's all skin!
Put it together, like you oughta…"
"Rumplestiltskin!" said the Miller's daughter.

"Boo, she's right!" shrieked the nasty imp.
He jumped up and down like a baby chimp.
He cried and sobbed and sucked his thumb,
"I hate that name! I could kill my mum!"

He stomped and stamped on the disco floor.
I went to throw him out the door,
But the Miller's Daughter shouted, "Stop!
That funky dwarf can really bop!"

"Show me the beat, my little man.
You dance better than the big boys can.
Come on, kids, make the party pump!
Get down, sisters! Do the rump!"

After that, the party chilled.
Poor Prince Thingy wasn't thrilled -
He lost his girl to the Stiltskin guy.
(He hid in the Gents and had a cry.)

I tell this story just to show
How wild these celebrations go.
If you have one, give me a shout -
You throw the party - I'll throw them out!

Written by Jeanne Willis * Illustrated by Korky Paul

All priced at £3.99 each

Crazy Jobs are available from all good book shops, or can be ordered direct
from the publisher: Orchard Books, PO BOX 29, Douglas IM99 1BQ
Credit card orders please telephone 01624 836000
or fax 01624 837033 or visit our Internet site: www.wattspub.co.uk
or e-mail: bookshop@enterprise.net for details.

To order please quote title, author and ISBN
and your full name and address.
Cheques and postal orders should be made payable to 'Bookpost plc.'
Postage and packing is FREE within the UK
(overseas customers should add £1.00 per book).
Prices and availability are subject to change.